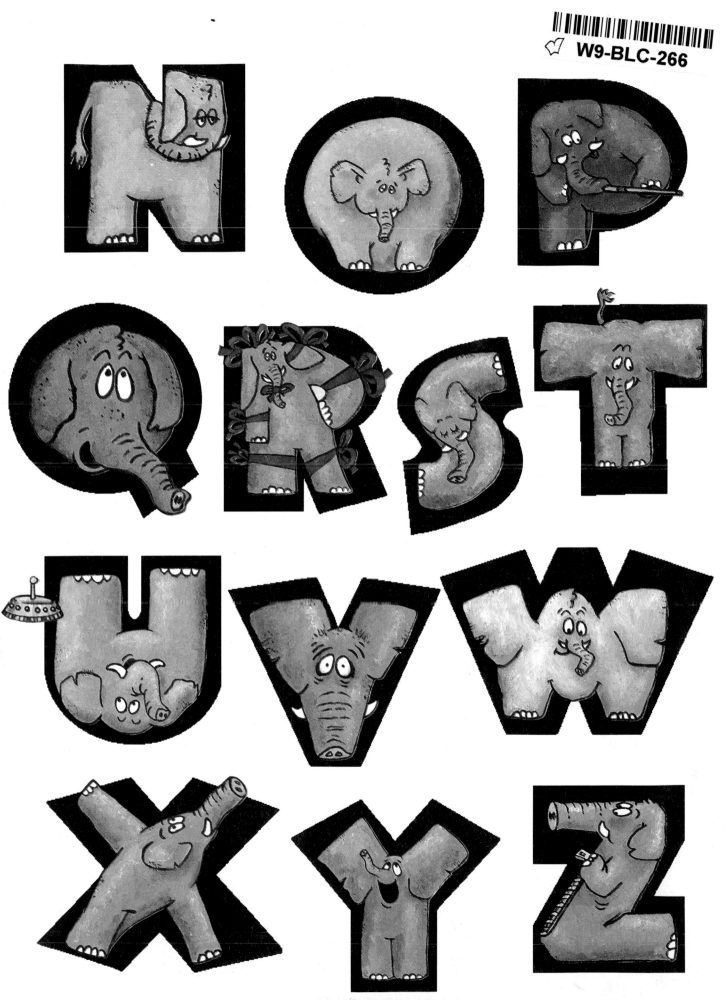

To my wife, Marie, my children Steve,
Risa, Dani, Doug, Dave and my grandchildren,
Cassi, Jessica, Nathan, Olivia, and Payden—
who encouraged my ideas.

Copyright © 1995 Gene Yates and Kidsbooks, Inc.
3535 West Peterson Avenue
Chicago, IL 60659

Printed in Canada
Hardcover edition bound in the United States of America

THE ELEPHANT ALPHABET BOOK

Written and Illustrated by
Gene Yates

A

A elephants want to be able Angels.

And they fly all alone in the air
up and down and all around.

B elephants like to buy Balloons.

And they turn blue when balloons are blown up so big that they burst with a bang!

C elephants enjoy catching Caterpillars.

And they can call cats, camels, and cockatoos, too.

D

D elephants like to draw Doodles.

And they do designs of
delightful dogs and dolls.

E

E **elephants have enormous Ears.**
And they easily eat everything eagerly.

F

F elephants
always fly Flags.

And they find
fantastic and
funny friends.

G

G elephants generally get Goofy.

And they turn green and get grumpy
whenever they gulp garlic.

H

H elephants are happy Helpers.

And they are happiest when they
help hold heavy handbags.

I elephants have iron-like Ivory tusks.

And they are into igloos made of ice.

J

J elephants jump for Joy.

And they like to jog while
eating jelly sandwiches
and drinking jugs of juice.

K

K elephants try to keep Kangaroos.

And they fly kites, eat ketchup, and
go to kindergarten.

L elephants really love Lilies.

And they like ladybugs, lazy lions,
and long lizards.

M

M elephants are afraid of mini-Mice.

And they love to move in murky,
mushy mud.

N

N elephants
have very nice Noses.

And they normally
wrap them around
their necks at night
to keep warm.

O

O elephants occasionally Overeat.

And they only
munch oranges,
oats, and olives.

Burp~

P elephants are skillful at playing Pool.

And they turn purple from
eating pink peas with pears.

Q

"My faithful, loyal subjects: I have gathered you here today ..."

Q elephants enjoy quoting Queens.

And they are quick to question quails and ducks that quack.

QUACK

QUACK

R

R elephants wear rosy red **Ribbons.**

And they like to race rabbits,
read books, and listen to radios.

S elephants are very sound Sleepers.

And they snore songs—sad songs,
simple songs, and silly songs.

T elephants spin tricky **Tops.**

And they talk to tigers and try other toys, too.

U

U elephants usually watch UFO's.

And they are unable to undo what ultimately turns them upside down ... unfortunately.

V

V elephants can be very Vocal.

And they like to raise their voices, take long voyages, and visit volcanoes.

W elephants enjoy watching Worms.

And they turn white when they wade in water, wallow in mud, or walk in the woods.

X elephants usually examine X rays.

And they are exact about extinct animals, with absolutely no exceptions!

Y

Y elephants like yelling "Yes!"

And they yackety-yack to young,
yellow canaries playing in their yard.

Z **elephants always zip up Zippers.**

And they visit zany zebras living in zoos.

TH  ND

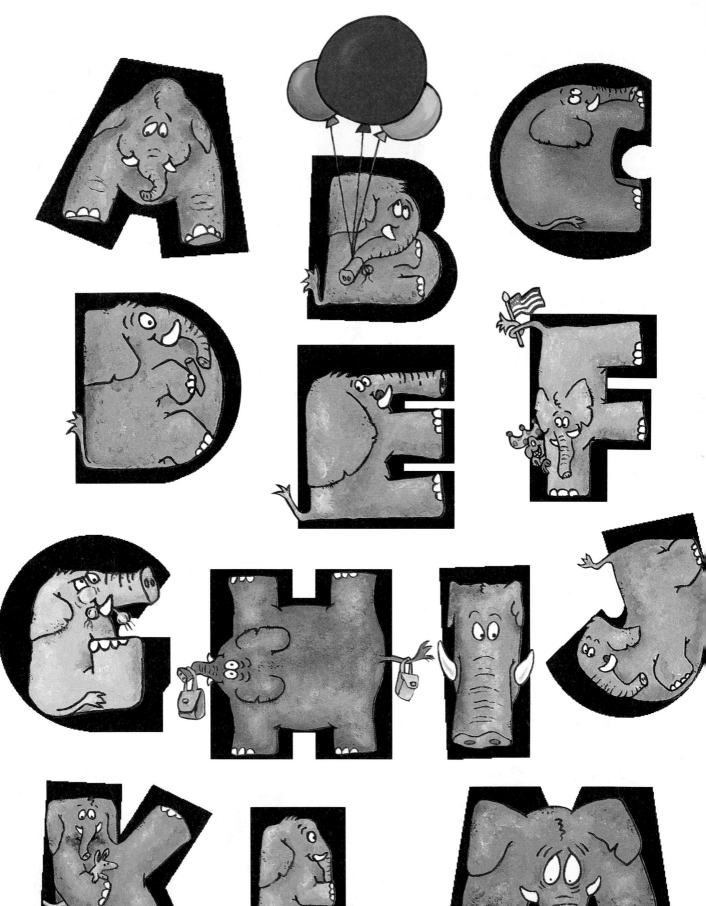